This igloo book belongs to:

....

igloobooks

Published in 2019
by Igloo Books Ltd
Cottage Farm
Sywell
NN6 0BJ
www.igloobooks.com

0819 001.01
2 4 6 8 10 9 7 5 3 1
ISBN 978-1-78905-670-9

Illustrated by Karen Sapp
Written by Rachel Elliot
Based on an original story by Kathryn Smith

Printed and manufactured in China

Just As I Am!

igloobooks

Little Elephant loves playing with his friends.
They run and jump and laugh together.
But today they can't think of any games to play.
Today they are just too hot.

"What shall we do?" asks Little Elephant.
"Play in the cool, shady spots," says his mother.

First, the friends play hide-and-seek. Lion Cub counts to ten.

"One... two... three..."

Crocodile hides in the water.
Monkey hides in a leafy tree.

Little Tiger hides in
the long, yellow grass.

But Little Elephant is too big.
He can't find anywhere to hide!

"**Ten!**" roars Lion Cub. "Ready or not, here I come!"
"There's nowhere for me to go!" cries Little Elephant.

He tries to hide behind a bush,
but his long trunk sticks out!

THUMP! BUMP! BANG!

Lion Cub trips over Little Elephant's trunk!

"Oops!" says Little Elephant. "I'm sorry."

"I don't want to play any more," sniffs Lion Cub.
Poor Little Elephant feels sad.
He didn't mean to spoil the game.

Next, the friends play tag. But Little Elephant is just too clumsy.

He can't see past his trunk, and bumps into Crocodile.
Monkey and Lion Cub have to leap out of the way!

"Let's play a different game," says Little Tiger.

So, they try playing ball. At first, they have lots of fun.
They run up and down, round and round!
Armadillo rolls all around the field.

But all that running around makes clouds of
dust, and the dust gets up Little Elephant's nose...

"AAAAACHOOOO!"

Little Elephant's sneeze blows Armadillo into the bushes!

"Sorry, Armadillo," mumbles Little Elephant.
"I think I'll go for a walk," he says, and he plods away by himself.

Little Elephant tries to make his trunk smaller,
but it's no use. He can't hide it.

Big tears roll down his face.

"What's the matter?" asks his mother, kindly.

"My trunk is too long," sniffs Little Elephant.
"It spoils all our games. I wish I could change!"

Little Elephant's mother wipes away his tears.

"Your trunk is very special," she says. "I know something you can play! Let's go and find your friends."

Then she whispers her plan in his ear.
Little Elephant's friends are splashing in the waterhole.

"This is boring!" says Little Tiger. Little Elephant smiles and fills his trunk with water. "Maybe I can help!" he cries.

SPLOOSH!

SPLASH!

Little Elephant trumpets water high
into the air and all over his friends.

"Fantastic!" laughs Lion Cub.

"Thanks, everyone!"
says Little Elephant.
"Now I'm happy...

... just as I am!"